HUGS & SHRUGS

The Continuing Saga of a Tiny Owl Named Squib

Written and Illustrated by

Larry Shles

Jalmar Press
45 Hitching Post Drive, Bldg. 2
Rolling Hills Estates, CA 90274-4297

Library of Congress Cataloging-in-Publication Data

Shles, Larry.
Hugs and Shrugs

Summary: Troubled because he feels incomplete
and has lost a piece of himself,
Squib searches his outside world
for it in vain.
He becomes complete again
once he discovers his own inner-peace.

[1. Fables.   2. Owls — Fiction.   3. Self-esteem — Fiction]
I. Title.   II. Title: Hugs & Shrugs
Library of Congress Catalog Card Number: 87-082162
ISBN: 0-915190-47-8
Printed in the United States of America

Cloth P Pbk. AL 10 9 8 7 6 5 4 3 2

To Carolyn who, too, knows this journey.

I also wish to thank Virginia Sapp and Becky Schroeder
for their continued belief and support.

Books by Larry Shles

Moths & Mothers, Feathers & Fathers

Hoots & Toots & Hairy Brutes

Hugs & Shrugs

HUGS & SHRUGS

The Continuing Saga of a
Tiny Owl Named Squib

Dawn melted away the darkness. Its misty glow illuminated the lush meadow and the secret crevices of the forest. But it didn't brighten Squib.

He awoke, empty and exhausted. Squib didn't feel happy. He didn't feel excited about the day.
His life no longer held any joy.

"Mom, I feel terrible," complained Squib. "I'm going back to bed."

"It's easy to see why you are unhappy," replied his mother. "Just look at your reflection in the pond."

Squib stared at his reflection. No wonder he felt incomplete, like a song without a last note. He had lost a piece of himself! Perhaps it had fallen out of his nest while he was sleeping.

Squib returned to the base of his tree.
He found several pieces, but none were his.

"Mom, my heart is like lead. I can't stand feeling this way. What should I do?"

"Just leave this to me," replied his mother. Not knowing what else to do, she began feeding him the odd-shaped pieces from under the nest.

"Mom, I don't think I'm supposed to eat these. And I feel like I'm going to explode."

"Just a few more, dear. Tomorrow you'll be as good as new."

The next morning Squib couldn't get his bulging stomach over the side of the nest. His empty space was as large as ever.

His mother's piece meal had been a total failure.

Life wasn't worth living if it felt like this. Squib resolved to go in search of the piece he had lost. Because he was just a small owl, unable to yet hoot or fly, he knew the journey would be difficult. Mustering all his energy, Squib left his nest and family and ventured into the world.

A short distance from his nest, Squib happened upon an owl suffering from a horrible malady. Birds must molt occasionally, but this unfortunate being was in a constant state of molt. Most of his feathers were gone and his oozy skin smelled like the entrance to a cave. The creature had a gaping space even larger than Squib's. A most remolting condition, Squib thought.

Not wanting to be bothered by such a useless creature, Squib tried to sneak by unnoticed.

"Will you hug me?" the creature murmured, catching Squib out of the corner of his eye.

Having more important matters to pursue, Squib shrugged and slinked on.

Turning from the creature, Squib heard the sounds of beautiful chanting. Other owls went to the sanctuary to find their eternal piece. Squib would do the same.

Seated on a comfortable yew, he prayed to the Owlmighty. "Please grant me everlasting piece." To Squib's dismay, nothing happened.

Perhaps there wasn't an Owlmighty after all. What if He were a different creature. Just in case, Squib offered up an oink. He even neighed to heaven. After a few half-hearted honks and snorts that went unanswered, Squib meekly departed, feeling confused and abandoned. He wondered, if there is an Owlmighty who cares, why doesn't He answer my prayers?

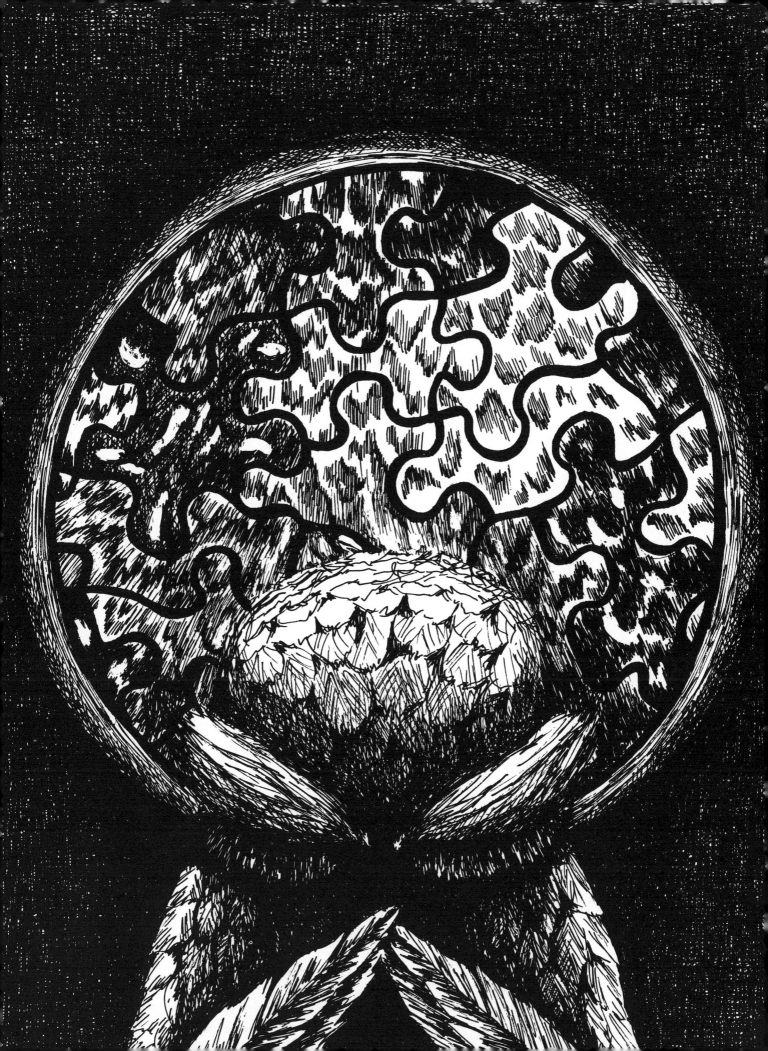

The clanging of the school bell cut through the stillness of the forest. Of course! Squib must have lost his piece of mind. He decided to search in his classroom.

"Your answer is in these books, Squib," his teacher exclaimed. "Understanding poetry will provide the path that leads to your piece. Read this poem and share its meaning with the class."

Squib stood and shared
his interpretation. Suddenly
he was interrupted. "That's ridiculous,
Squib," chided this teacher. "I will
tell the class what the poem really means."

"Yes, but my idea…"

"I don't need to hear any more of your
idea. You're obviously not yet a poet or a
scholar. I will teach you the truth."

"But I want to know my truth," pleaded
Squib.

With that, the teacher went into a rage. In
a fearful display, she spread her plumage and
shooed Squib from the class.

The teacher had given Squib a piece of her
own mind.

Muddling on, Squib happened upon a powerful owl perched on an enormous pedestal.

Squib spoke in a particularly tiny toot. "Great and special sir, you have been to every corner of the forest. Have you by chance seen the piece of me that I have lost?"

The imposing bird looked disdainfully at Squib. "You're mighty young, boy. Why don't you come back when you're a little older? I'll help you when you can help me."

The bird then turned its head around and stared at the sky. For the first time, Squib noticed how ridiculous an owl looks when it faces you and faces away at the same time.

A mountain loomed majestically in front of Squib. Other owls sought fulfillment in challenge and competition. Some pursued flight endurance records; others sought a record number of mates in a year. Squib would seek his completion by conquering the mountain.

He began his ascent with great hope and enthusiasm. Soon the rocks became steep; the wind became angry. Squib found himself clinging to a sheer cliff face. Somehow he found a wing tip hold. He crept, painstakingly, upward.

Squib never reached the top. Part way up into the foothills, he found what seemed to be a magic box. He became glued to the images of other owls and their exploits. Content to watch, he set aside his own quest for the summit.

For months he followed the fate of his heroes. He lived and died with their successes and failures.

At the end of the season his team had won only one game and had lost fourteen. With the final buzzer, Squib came unglued and went to pieces.

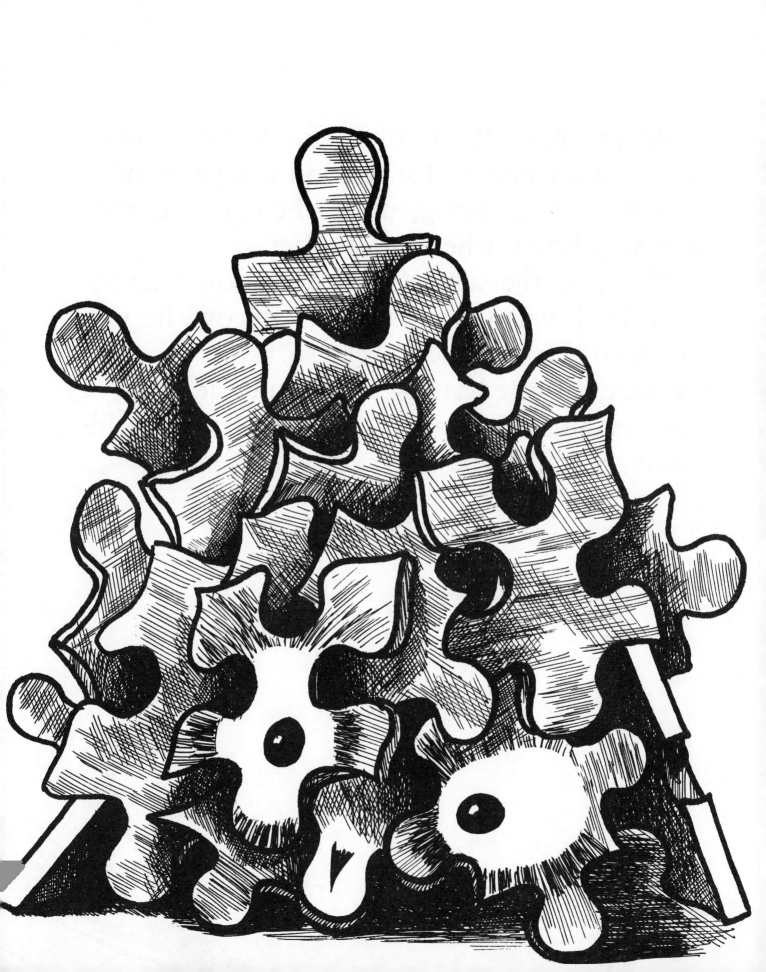

Pulling himself together, Squib descended to the valley below. He was on the verge of accepting his gnawing, unfinished feeling and returning home when he saw her.

Sitting in the seed strands of a towering thorn bush was the most beautiful owl he had ever seen. Her feathers were soft and inviting; her gaze reflected landscapes Squib couldn't even imagine. If there was a completion to his puzzle, it had to be up there with her.

Squib caught her attention with his clearest toot. He displayed his plumage and strutted like a rooster.

"Look at me! Look at me!" he thought, hoping beyond hope.

To his surprise, she smiled and motioned for him to join her. Ecstatic, Squib rushed to the prickly stem and began his climb. He paid no attention to the terrifying thorns that pointed the way toward her.

At length he reached the silky fuzziness of her nest overlooking the meadow. Tentatively, he approached the beautiful owl. She spread her magnificent wings and wrapped herself around him. Squib returned her embrace.

He sensed his empty feeling drifting away. His body filled with a joy he had never known. Clinging together for weeks, they shared soft words and stories of their own journeys.

Squib would never have to search again. What a life he could anticipate!

One morning, Squib was awakened by a cold draft. She was gone! He scanned the meadow. There was no trace of her. He waited, the emptiness growing larger with the passage of each day. For weeks he remained alone, alert to even the slightest hint that she was returning.

She never did. Squib never found out why she had gone. He remained motionless for a long time. The emptiness inside had grown. It had even brimmed over, filling his body and extending beyond.

Anxious to return home, Squib began his climb down to the world below. Now the thorns were aimed directly at him. Halfway down the stem, he lost his grip. With a plop he returned to earth, bruised and bleeding.

"I knew I should have ended my search and gone back home long ago. Now there's little left of me." Squib's empty space was dark and heavy; it had no beginning and no end. He felt as lonely as all of space.

"I need someone to hold me," Squib thought. "I need someone to plug up my space so the rest of me won't drain away before I get home."

The vulture was not a great candidate for a hug, but he happened to be around. "I'm on my way home. I feel like I'm about to die. Will you hug me?" Squib asked.

"You're on your way home to die, huh Squib?" remarked the vulture with sudden interest. "I'll be happy to hug you, but not right now. Don't call me. I'll call you."

Staggering on, Squib encountered a bat hanging from a branch. "You have wings that could envelop me. Will you hug me?" Squib asked.

"With pleasure," the bat replied. "However, you will have to hang from the branch with me."

Squib had never tried hanging from a branch before. He got out on the limb and valiantly swung downward. As Squib plummeted to earth, the bat grinned and grew taller in a low-down way.

Plodding on, Squib happened upon a hummingbird. "Will you hug me?" pleaded Squib.

"Can't you see how busy I am?" whirred the hummingbird. "Do you have any idea how many times I have to beat my wings per second just to stay in one place? I can't take time to hug you. Besides, I'd waste too much energy getting revved up again."

The wolf looked cuddly. His neck fur was full and fluffy. "Will you hug me?" implored Squib.

"There was a time when I could have given you the greatest hug," explained the wolf. "There was a time when I was warm. But for many years I have been the only wolf left in this forest. The loneliness has taken a great toll. I have nothing left to give."

Disbelieving, Squib snuggled down into the wolf's thickest fur, eagerly awaiting the reassuring touch. He was startled by the unyielding skin. It was as stiff as a marble slab.

The golden eagle, regal and stunning, loomed in front of Squib. "I'm in terrible need of a hug. Will you hold me?" pleaded Squib.

"You've got to be kidding, runt," blurted the eagle. "Can't you see that I am the most beautiful and glamorous creature in the world? I can hug any animal I want. I certainly don't want to hug you. After all, I am greatness. What are you?"

Desperation prevailed as Squib neared the snake. He sensed great danger, but his need to be comforted was overwhelming. Squib climbed into one of the snake's coils. "Will you hug me? Even a little squeeze would be all right."

"With great pleasure, Squib! You are truly a piéce de resistance!"

The snake's body began to tighten. Feeling all the blood being squeezed into his head, Squib realized this was no ordinary hug. With surprising resolve, he popped loose and fled to safety.

Squeezed, battered and exhausted,
Squib neared the last bend in the path
before home. Suddenly he detected a
familiar musty smell.

Squib found himself face to face with the wretched, remolting bird. He felt no need to sneak by. He was no longer disgusted by the sight of this unfortunate being. He felt a powerful force pulling him toward the mass of wrinkled skin.

He crawled up on the lap of the bird. He found himself peering directly into its gaping space. In the darkness within, Squib found his own reflection. Slowly he spread his wings. The urge to embrace this woeful being overwhelmed him. Squib pulled himself as close as he could to the creature's body and pressed tightly.

He felt the creature's warm tears trickle onto his head. Squib was at once able to breathe more freely. He looked down and discovered that his gap had been filled. Squib let the warmth and joy surround him.

He understood now. His piece had not fallen out at all. It had fallen in. It was his inner piece. All beings must have these spaces of loneliness and pain, Squib thought.

Needing only acceptance, Squib's piece re-surfaced from within.

With ease, Squib climbed up the wing of the creature and rested on his shoulder. The view was breathtaking.

Squib had never felt this way before. Sensations of freedom and exhaltation lingered and consumed him in warmth and light.

Squib's journey had brought him, at last, to the loftiest perch he could ever know. He was home.

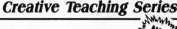

Learning The Skills of Peacemaking
An Activity Guide for Elementary-Age Children

"Global peace begins with you. Guide develops this fundamental concept in fifty lessons. If this curriculum was a required course in every elementary school in every country, we would see world peace in our children's lifetimes." — *Letty Cottin Pogrebin*, Ms. Magazine
0-915190-46-X $21.95
8½ × 11   paperback, illus.

Project Self-Esteem EXPANDED
A Parent Involvement Program for Elementary-Age Children

An innovative parent-support program that promotes children's self-worth. "Project Self Esteem is the most extensively tested and affordable drug and alcohol preventative program available."

0-915190-59-1 $39.95
8½ × 11   paperback, illus.

The Two Minute Lover
Announcing A New Idea In Loving Relationships

No one is foolish enough to imagine that s/he *automatically* deserves success. Yet, almost everyone thinks that they automatically deserve sudden and continuous success in marriage. Here's a book that helps make that belief a reality.
0-915190-52-4 $9.95
6 × 9   paperback, illus.

Reading, Writing and Rage

An autopsy of one profound school failure, disclosing the complex processes behind it and the secret rage that grew out of it.

Must reading for anyone working with learning disabled, functional illiterates, or juvenile delinquents.

0-915190-42-7 $16.95
5½ × 8½   paperback

Feel Better Now
30 Ways to Handle Frustrations in Three Minutes or Less

A practical menu of instant stress reduction techniques, designed to be used right in the middle of high-pressure situations. Feel Better Now includes stress management tools for every problem and every personality style.
0-915190-66-4 $9.95
6 × 9 paperback, appendix, biblio.

Esteem Builders

You CAN improve your students' behavior and achievement through building self-esteem. Here is a book packed with classroom- proven techniques, activities, and ideas you can immediately use in your own program or at home.

Ideas, ideas, ideas, for grades K-8 and parents.

0-915190-53-2 $39.95
8½ × 11   paperback, illus.

Good Morning Class—I Love You!
Thoughts and Questions About Teaching from the Heart

A book that helps create the possibility of having schools be places where students, teachers and principals get what every human being wants and needs—LOVE!

0-915190-58-3 $6.95
5½ × 8½ paperback, illus.

I am a blade of grass
A Breakthrough in Learning and Self-Esteem

Help your students become "lifetime learners," empowered with the confidence to make a positive difference in their world (without abandoning discipline or sacrificing essential skill and content acquisition).
0-915190-54-0 $14.95
6 × 9   paperback, illus.

Unlocking Doors to Self-Esteem

Presents innovative ideas to make the secondary classroom a more positive learning experience—socially and emotionally—for students and teachers. Over 100 lesson plans included. Designed for easy infusion into curriculum. Gr. 7-12

0-915190-60-5 $16.95
6 × 9 paperback, illus

SAGE: *Self-Awareness Growth Experiences*

A veritable treasure trove of activities and strategies promoting positive behavior and meeting the personal/social needs of young people in grades 7-12. Organized around affective learning goals and objectives. Over 150 activities.
0-915190-61-3 $16.95
6 × 9 paperback, illus.

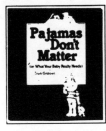

Pajamas Don't Matter:
(or What Your Baby Really Needs)

Here's help for new parents every-
where! Provides valuable information
and needed reassurances to new
parents as they struggle through the
frantic, but rewarding, first years of
their child's life.
0-915190-21-4 $5.95
8½ × 11   paperback, full color

Why Does Santa Celebrate Christmas?

What do wisemen, shepherds and
angels have to do with Santa,
reindeer and elves? Explore this
Christmas fantasy which ties all of
the traditions of Christmas into one
lovely poem for children of all
ages.
0-915190-67-2 $12.95
8 1/2 x 11 hardcover, full color

Feelings Alphabet

Brand-new kind of alphabet book full
of photos and word graphics that will
delight readers of all ages.". . . lively,
candid. . .the 26 words of
this pleasant book express
experiences common to all children."
Library Journal
0-935266-15-1 $7.95
6 × 9   paperback, B/W photos

The Parent Book

A functional and sensitive guide for
parents who want to enjoy every min-
ute of their child's growing years.
Shows how to live with children in
ways that encourage healthy emo-
tional development. Ages 3-14.
0-915190-15-X $9.95
8½ × 11   paperback, illus.

Aliens In My Nest
SQUIB Meets The Teen Creature

Squib comes home from summer
camp to find that his older brother,
Andrew, has turned into a snarly,
surly, defiant, and non-communica-
tive adolescent. *Aliens* explores the
effect of Andrew's new behavior on
Squib and the entire family unit.
0-915190-49-4 $7.95
8½ × 11   paperback, illus.

Hugs & Shrugs
The Continuing Saga of SQUIB

Squib feels incomplete. He has lost a
piece of himself. He searches every
where only to discover that his miss-
ing piece has fallen in and not out.
He becomes complete again once
he discovers his own inner-peace.

0-915190-47-8 $7.95
8½ × 11   paperback, illus.

Moths & Mothers/
Feather & Fathers
*A Story About a Tiny Owl
Named SQUIB*

Squib is a tiny owl who cannot fly.
Neither can he understand his feelings. He must face the frustration,
grief, fear, guilt and loneliness that
we all must face at different times in
our lives. Struggling with these feelings, he searches, at least, for
understanding.

0-915190-57-5 $7.95
8½ × 11   paperback, illus.

Hoots & Toots & Hairy Brutes
*The Continuing Adventures
of SQUIB*

Squib—who can only toot—sets out
to learn how to give a mighty hoot.
His attempts result in abject failure.
Every reader who has struggled with
life's limitations will recognize their
own struggles and triumphs in the
microcosm of Squib's forest world. A
parable for all ages from 8 to 80.

0-915190-56-7 $7.95
8½ × 11   paperback, illus.

Do I Have To Go To School Today?
Squib Measures Up!

Squib dreads the daily task of going
to school. In this volume, he
daydreams about all the reasons he
has not to go. But, in the end, Squib
convinces himself to go to school
because his teacher accepts him
"Just as he is!"

0-915190-62-1 $7.95
8½ × 11   paperback, illus.

The Turbulent Teens
Understanding Helping Surviving

"This book should be read by every
parent of a teenager in America. . .It
gives a parent the information
needed to understand teenagers and
guide them wisely."—Dr. Fitzhugh
Dodson, author of *How to Parent,
How to Father, and How to Discipline
with Love.*
0-913091-01-4 $8.95
6 × 9   paperback.

Openmind/Wholemind
Parenting & Teaching Tomorrow's Children Today

A book of powerful possibilities that honors the capacities, capabilities, and potentials of adult and child alike. Uses Modalities, Intelligences, Styles and Creativity to explore how the brain-mind system acquires, processes and expresses experience. Foreword by M. McClaren & C. Charles.
0-915190-45-1 $14.95
7 × 9   paperback
81 B/W photos   29 illus.

Present Yourself! *Captivate Your Audience With Great Presentation Skills*

Become a presenter who is a dynamic part of the message. Learn about Transforming Fear, Knowing Your Audience, Setting The Stage, Making Them Remember and much more. Essential reading for anyone interested in the art of communication. Destined to become the standard work in its field.
0-915190-51-6   paper $9.95
0-915190-50-8   cloth $18.95
6 × 9   paper/cloth. illus.

Unicorns Are Real
A Right-Brained Approach to Learning

Over 100,000 sold. The long-awaited "right hemispheric" teaching strategies developed by popular educational specialist Barbara Vitale are now available. Hemispheric dominance screening instrument included.
0-915190-35-4 $12.95
8½ × 11   paperback, illus.

Unicorns Are Real Poster

Beautifully-illustrated. Guaranteed to capture the fancy of young and old alike. Perfect gift for unicorn lovers, right-brained thinkers and all those who know how to dream. For classroom, office or home display.

JP9027 $4.95
19 × 27   full color

NEW

Metaphoric Mind (Revised Ed.)
Here is a plea for a balanced way of thinking and being in a culture that stands on the knife-edge between catastrophe and transformation. The metaphoric mind is asking again, quietly but insistently, for equilibrium. For, after all, equilibrium is the way of nature.
0-915190-68-0 $14.95
7 × 10 paperback, B/W photos

Don't Push Me, I'm Learning as Fast as I Can

Barbara Vitale presents some remarkable insights on the physical growth stages of children and how these stages affect a child's ability, not only to learn, but to function in the classroom.
JP9112 $12.95
Audio Cassette

Tapping Our Untapped Potential

This Barbara Vitale tape gives new insights on how you process information. Will help you develop strategies for improving memory, fighting stress and organizing your personal and professional activities.

JP9111 $12.95
Audio Cassette

Free Flight *Celebrating Your Right Brain*

Journey with Barbara Vitale, from her uncertain childhood perceptions of being "different" to the acceptance and adult celebration of that difference. A book for right-brained people in a left-brained world. Foreword by Bob Samples.
0-915190-44-3 $9.95
5½ × 8½   paperback, illus.

"He Hit Me Back First"
Self-Esteem through Self-Discipline

Simple techniques for guiding children toward self-correcting behavior as they become aware of choice and their own inner authority.
0-915190-36-2 $12.95
8½ × 11   paperback, illus.

Learning To Live, Learning To Love

An inspirational message about the importance of love in everything we do. Beautifully told through words and pictures. Ageless and timeless.
0-915190-38-9 $7.95
6 × 9   paperback, illus.

TA For Tots
(and other prinzes)

Over 500,000 sold.

This innovative book has helped thousands of young children and their parents to better understand and relate to each other. Ages 4-9.
0-915190-12-5 $12.95
8½ × 11   paper, color, illus.

TA For Tots, Vol. II

Explores new ranges of feelings and suggests solutions to problems such as feeling hurt, sad, shy, greedy, or lonely.

Ages 4-9.

0-915190-25-7 $12.95
8½ × 11   paper, color, illus.

TA for Kids
(and grown-ups too)

Over 250,000 sold.

The message of TA is presented in simple, clear terms so youngsters can apply it in their daily lives. Warm Fuzzies abound. Ages 9-13.
0-915190-09-5 $9.95
8½ × 11   paper, color, illus.

TA For Teens
(and other important people)

Over 100,000 sold.

Using the concepts of Transactional Analysis. Dr. Freed explains the ups and downs of adulthood without talking down to teens. Ages 13-18.
0-915190-03-6 $18.95
8½ × 11   paperback, illus.

Original Warm Fuzzy Tale *Learn about "Warm Fuzzies" firsthand.*

Over 100,000 sold.

A classic fairytale . . . with adventure, fantasy, heroes, villains and a moral. Children (and adults, too) will enjoy this beautifully illustrated book.

0-915190-08-7 $7.95
6 × 9   paper, full color, illus.

Songs of The Warm Fuzzy
"All About Your Feelings"

The album includes such songs as Hitting is Harmful, Being Scared, When I'm Angry, Warm Fuzzy Song, Why Don't Parents Say What They Mean, and I'm Not Perfect (Nobody's Perfect).
JP9003 $12.95
                Cassette

Tot Pac *(Audio-Visual Kit)*

Includes 5 filmstrips, 5 cassettes, 2 record LP album. A *Warm Fuzzy I'm OK* poster, 8 coloring posters, 10 Warm Fuzzies. 1 *TA for Tots* and 92 page *Leader's Manual.* No prior TA training necessary to use Tot Pac in the classroom! Ages 2-9.
JP9032 $150.00
Multimedia program

Kid Pac *(Audio-Visual Kit)*

Teachers, counselors, and parents of pre-teens will value this easy to use program. Each *Kid Pac* contains 13 cassettes, 13 filmstrips, 1 *TA For Kids,* and a comprehensive *Teacher's Guide,* plus 10 Warm Fuzzies. Ages 9-13.
JP9033 $195.00
Multimedia Program

B.L. Winch & Assoc./Jalmar Press
45 Hitching Post Dr., Bldg. 2
Rolling Hills Estates, CA 90274

CALL TOLL FREE: 800/662-9662
In California, Call Collect: 213/547-1240

Please Enclose Check or
Credit Card Information

NAME _____

STREET ADDRESS OR R.F.D. _____

CITY/STATE/ZIP _____

☐ Charge to VISA/MC   ☐ Acct. # _____ Exp. Date _____

Cardholder's Signature _____

TITLE	QTY	UNIT PRICE	TOTAL

Sub-Total: _____
CA Sales Tax: _____
Add 10% Shipping/Handling (**Min. $3.00**): _____
TOTAL: _____